THERE WAS AN OLD LADY WHO SWALLOWED SOME LEAVES!

by Lucille Colandro
Illustrated by Jared Lee

Cartwheel
·B·O·O·K·S·®

SCHOLASTIC INC.
New York Toronto London Auckland
Sydney Mexico City New Delhi Hong Kong

With love for Penny, Bob,
Erica, and Jonathan.
— L.C.

To Mike and Amy Luke
— J.L.

ISBN 978-0-545-24198-4

Text copyright © 2010 by Lucille Colandro.
Illustrations copyright © 2010 by Jared D. Lee Studios.

23 22 21 20 19 18 17   17 18 19/0

Printed in the U.S.A.   40
This edition first printing, August 2010

There was an old lady who swallowed some leaves.
I don't know why she swallowed those leaves.
Perhaps she'll sneeze!

There was an old lady who swallowed a shirt.
It didn't hurt to swallow that shirt.

She swallowed the shirt to fill it with leaves.
I don't know why she swallowed the leaves.
Perhaps she'll sneeze!

There was an old lady who swallowed a pumpkin.
She wasn't a bumpkin to swallow that pumpkin.

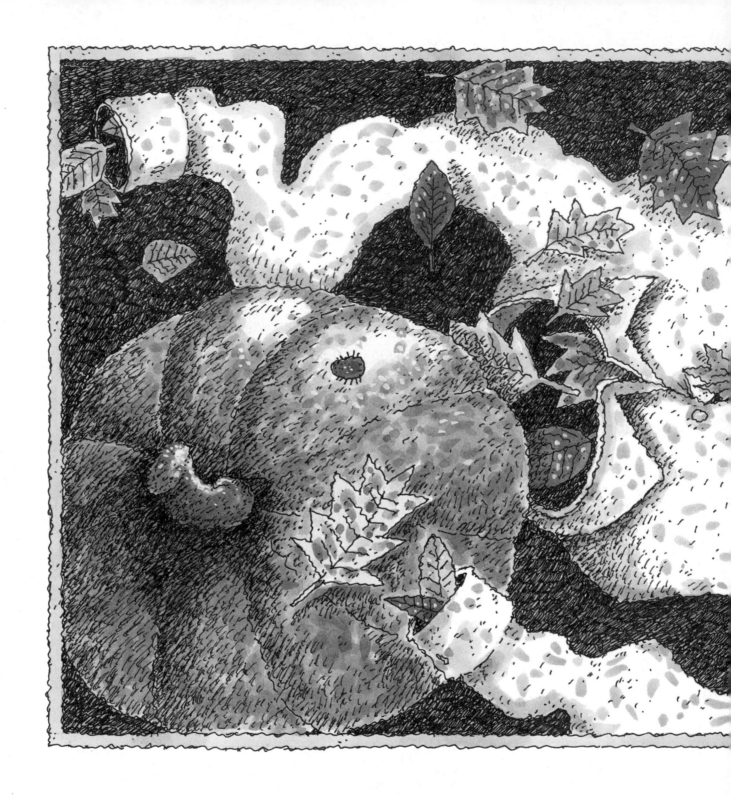

She swallowed the pumpkin to wear the shirt.
She swallowed the shirt to fill it with leaves.

I don't know why she swallowed the leaves.
Perhaps she'll sneeze!

There was an old lady who swallowed a pole.

She was on a roll when she swallowed that pole.

She swallowed the pole to prop up the pumpkin.
She swallowed the pumpkin to wear the shirt.
She swallowed the shirt to fill it with leaves.

I don't know why she swallowed the leaves.
Perhaps she'll sneeze!

There was an old lady who swallowed some pants.

She started to dance when she swallowed the pants.

She swallowed the pants to cover the pole.
She swallowed the pole to prop up the pumpkin.
She swallowed the pumpkin to wear the shirt.

She swallowed the shirt to fill it with leaves.
I don't know why she swallowed the leaves.
Perhaps she'll sneeze!

There was an old lady who swallowed a rope.
She didn't mope when she swallowed that rope.

She swallowed the rope to tie up the pants.

She swallowed the pants to cover the pole.

She swallowed the pole to prop up the pumpkin.

She swallowed the pumpkin to wear the shirt.

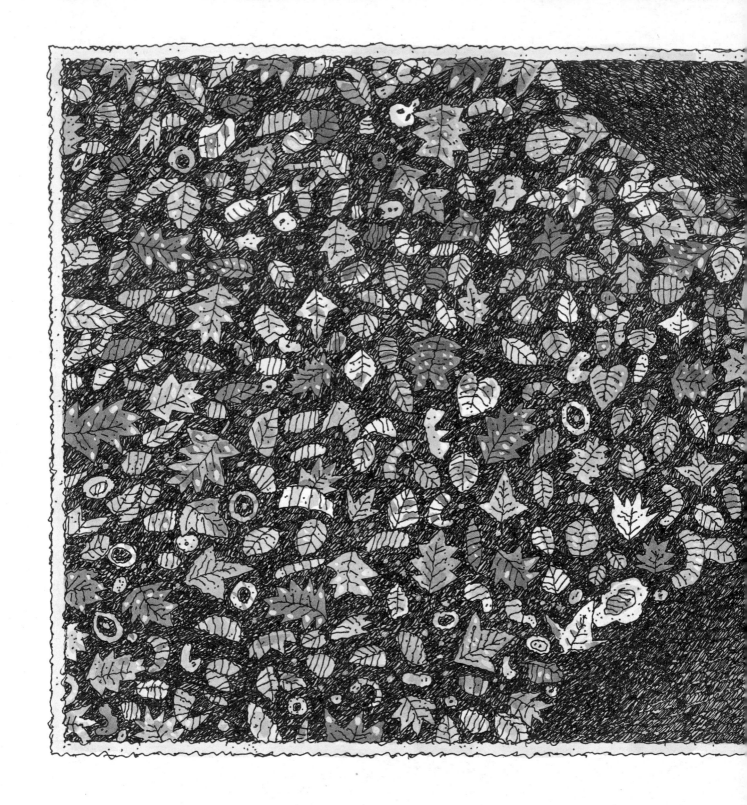

She swallowed the shirt to fill it with leaves.

Happy fall!

There was an old lady who swallowed some hay.

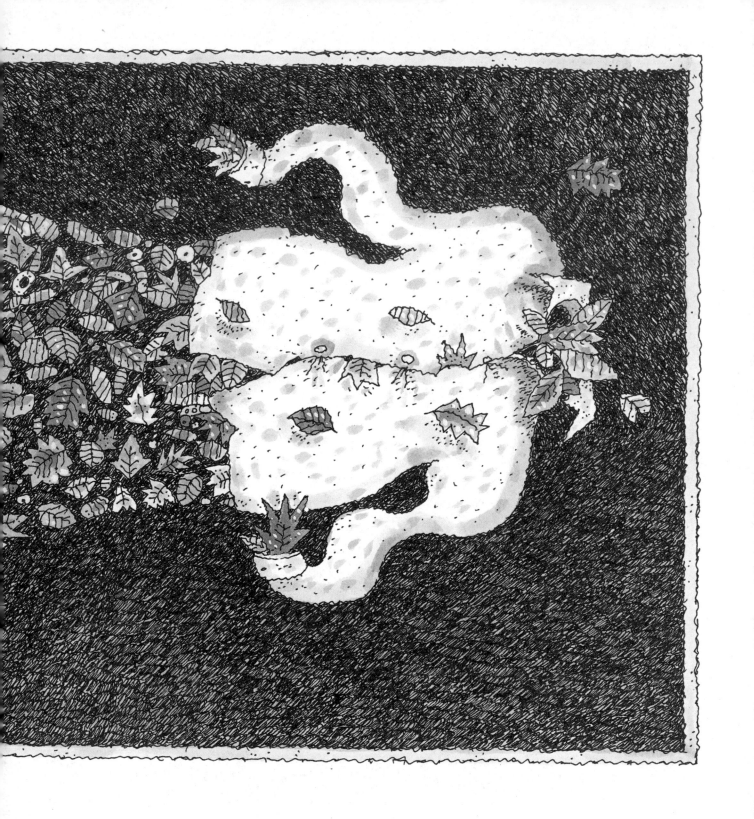

I don't know why she swallowed the leaves.
Perhaps she'll sneeze!

She didn't say why she swallowed that hay.

But she did it with ease
and then she started to sneeze—